The Dinosaur Friend

Steggy

Trisha

Tyro

Bronty

Share the Amazing Adventures of
Bronty Brontosaurus and His Friends

by Stewart Cowley

Grange
BOOKS

Published in 1999 by **Grange Books, a**n imprint of Grange Books Plc,
The Grange, Units 1-6, Kingsnorth Industrial Estate, Hoo, Nr. Rochester, Kent ME3 9ND

ISBN 1 84013 347 3

Printed in Singapore

THREE EXCITING STORIES

Bronty Saves the Day

One day Bronty woke up very late. He yawned and stuck his head out from the bushes. 'It's a good day for an adventure,' he thought. He crawled out of his nest and peered around, turning his long, long neck from left to right. 'I wonder where my friends are?'

He looked everywhere for the other baby dinosaurs. He looked in the swamp where they loved to splash in the warm, shallow water. He searched the hot springs where they sometimes rolled in the soft, squishy mud. He even trudged all the way up Fire Mountain;

7

but there was no sign of them.

'They've gone somewhere without me,' thought Bronty gloomily. 'I'm going to sulk in the forest.'

As he stomped through the trees, he heard distant laughter. Bronty started to gallop towards the noise. The ground trembled under his weight and trees crashed aside as he thundered along.

He burst into the open in a shower of branches and leaves, and skidded to a sudden halt.

'Well done, Bronty!' his friends cried. 'You've been a big help.'

Bronty looked puzzled. 'Have I?' he asked. Steggy grinned. 'We couldn't find enough wood to finish our raft. Now we have plenty, thanks to you!' There were broken branches scattered everywhere from Bronty's charge through the forest. They collected the wood, and set to work. Soon the boat was in the water and all the dinosaur friends climbed aboard. 'Right, everybody paddle,' said

Steggy. They paddled and splashed and splashed and paddled, but the boat refused to move.

'It's you, Bronty,' said Trisha. 'You're too heavy! The boat is touching the bottom. You'll have to push us off.' 'It's not my fault that I'm big,' grumbled

Bronty as he climbed out of the boat.

Bronty gave a huge push. The boat shot straight out into the middle of the stream, and Bronty fell head first into the water. He struggled to his feet, coughing and spluttering, as the boat picked up speed in the fast current.

'Wait for me!' wailed Bronty. 'We can't stop,' shouted the others, as Bronty ran after them, 'the river's too strong! We're paddling as fast as we can but the current's keeping us in the middle.'

As Bronty ran, he heard a strange rumbling, hissing sound that was growing louder. Ahead, part of the river bank jutted out into the stream. 'If I can get there before the boat, perhaps I could jump aboard,' he thought. As he ran ahead of the boat, he realized what the funny noise was. 'Oh no!' he gasped.

'It's a huge waterfall, and they are heading straight for it!'

Bronty ran faster than he had ever run before. He reached the point of land as the boat approached, and hurled himself into the water. 'Throw me a vine quickly,' he yelled.

The roar of the waterfall was deafening as the terrified friends threw the vine. Bronty grabbed it in his mouth and struggled back to the the bank.

'Hurrah for Bronty!' shouted his friends. 'You have saved us from a very nasty accident.'

The Forbidden Place

All the baby dinos were bored. They had planned to have a barbecue on Fire Mountain, but the sky had turned gloomy, and a thick haze of smoke and steam covered the peak of the volcano. 'My mother says I'm not to go up Fire Mountain today,' sighed Tyro.

'So did mine,' said Bronty. 'What can we do instead?' 'Well,' said Steggy, 'we must find somewhere else to have our barbecue.'

The four pals gathered up their bundles of food, and set off. After a while, they came to the Rocky Maze, a place of ravines, huge boulders and craggy pillars of rock. It was the farthest from their homes that they were allowed to go. When they reached the end, they looked out at the

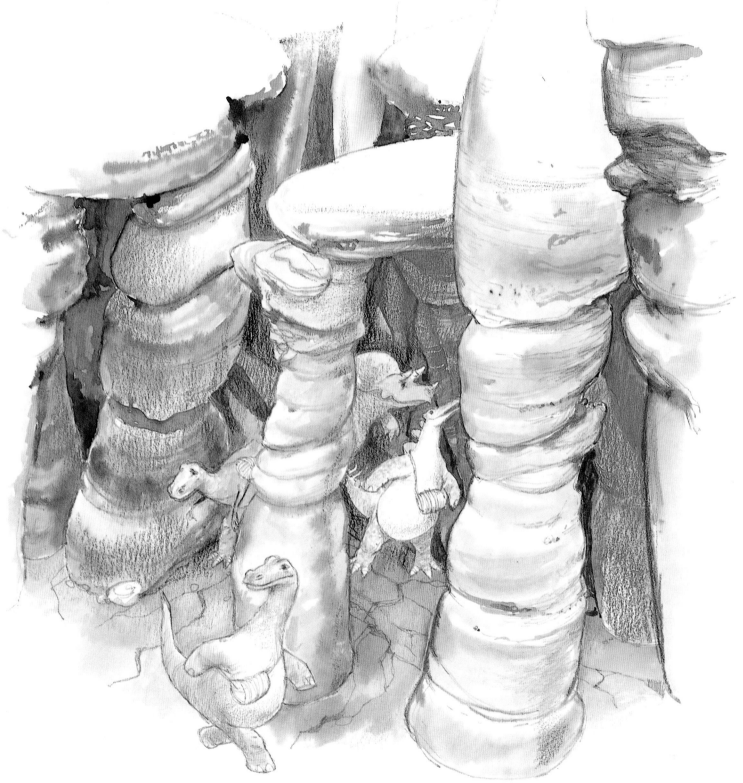

forbidden country beyond. 'I...I...I'm a bit scared,' whispered Tyro. 'I think we should go back home now.'

'Nonsense!' snapped Steggy. 'If you are exploring, it has to be somewhere new. Come on!' The ground was rough, and wisps of steam rose from hundred of cracks in the ground. After a while, Tyro whispered,' I want to go home.' 'Alright', said Bronty, 'I'll take you.' 'We're not scared,' said Trisha and Steggy, 'we're going on.'

As Bronty led Tyro away, he kept

looking back. Suddenly he stopped. 'Something's happening!' There was a deep rumbling, and a jet of flame flared from the distant shape of Fire Mountain. 'It's an eruption!' gasped Tyro, 'and an earthquake!'

Through the dusty air, they could see Steggy and Trisha running back. Then the cracks in the ground opened wider and suddenly Steggy and Trisha vanished. 'Quick!' Bronty bellowed. 'We've got to save them!' 'I think the

earthquake's over,' panted Tyro, 'but where are the others?' 'We're down here!' came a faint cry. Bronty skidded to a stop, and peered over the edge of a deep crack. There were Steggy and Trisha at the bottom. 'We're alright,' they sobbed, 'but we can't get out!'

The sides were very steep, but Bronty could see a ledge about halfway down. 'Even if I could get to that ledge,' he thought, 'I still won't be able to reach them.' 'Have you got a plan, Bronty?' asked Tyro. 'Um...maybe...nearly,' answered Bronty. 'But if you have an

idea, I don't mind if you tell it to me.' Tyro thought for a moment. 'I don't know how to get them out, but I do know that the edge of the crack just doesn't look very safe.'

He was right. As he spoke, Bronty suddenly felt the soil move beneath him. 'Look out!' yelled Tyro. 'It's giving way!' Bronty tried to jump clear, but down he plummeted, over and over, in a huge landslide of earth and stones. 'Ooof!' went Bronty, as he landed on the ledge below. He covered his head as the landslide rumbled and crashed

past him. 'Are you alright, Bronty?' asked Tyro. 'I think so,' Bronty answered. Suddenly a familiar voice said, 'That was a very good plan!' It gave Bronty quite a fright. 'Steggy! Trisha! How did you get up here?' Steggy laughed. 'When you pushed all that stuff down in a big heap, it was easy to climb up here. Wasn't that your plan?' Bronty blushed. 'Er...well...hmm...not exactly,' he stuttered. 'But at least it worked. Now we just have to get off this ledge.' 'That's easy,' said Tyro from above

them. 'I'll hang my tail over the edge and you can pull yourselves up.'

Once they were all out, they set off for home.

'The next time I feel bored,' said Bronty with a laugh, 'I'm going to have a nap instead of deciding to explore forbidden places.'

Bronty's New Game

Bronty was full of energy. 'This is a day for doing everything very fast.' He started to run, and when he came across some small rocks, he jumped over them, one after another. 'Whee!' he cried. 'This is half galloping and half jumping. I shall call it gallumping!' As he gallumped, the ground shook and the rocks bounced and rattled at every step. 'I must show my friends,' thought Bronty.

'It's hot. I'll bet they are in the swamp,' thought Bronty, as he gullumped along; and he was right. Trisha, Steggy and Tyro were lying around on the cool grass in the shade of the palm trees. They were snoozing when Bronty arrived. 'Yoohoo! Look at me!' he bellowed, as he gullumped through the shallow water. Great fountains of mud exploded into the air whenever he landed. 'Aaargh! Go away Bronty!' the others roared as the mud

23

began to splatter them.

When Bronty stopped gullumping, he looked around proudly. But his friends had run away to escape the shower of mud. 'That's funny!' said Bronty. 'Where can they have gone.' He thought for a moment. 'They are probably in the forest.' Bronty walked to the forest, but when he heard his friends' voices, he took a deep breath and gallumped towards them as fast as he could. The trees shook and shivered and leaves

showered down from the branches.

'Oh no! He's doing that thing again!' wailed his friends. The air was filled with whirling leaves and twigs as Bronty slid to a halt. He couldn't see a thing as the leaves drifted down; but when the air cleared, he was alone. 'Huh! Where did they go? I was certain that they were here.' He looked around and saw tracks leading out of the clearing. 'It looks as though they ran away,' thought Bronty. 'Something must have frightened them.'

Bronty followed the tracks, practising his gallumping as he went. He left the forest and eventually spotted three distant shapes sitting in the shelter of a large rock. 'There they are!' he chuckled. 'Now I'll show them.' He took a deep breath. 'Here we goooo!' he rumbled, as he gallumped at full speed towards them. The ground shook, and a huge dust cloud surrounded him as he sped along.

'Oh No!' chorused Trisha, Steggy and Tyro. 'Here he comes again!' The huge dust cloud was hurtling straight towards them, and the pounding of Bronty's feet grew louder. When he slid to a stop, Bronty looked around with a big grin. 'How about that!' he beamed. 'That's called gallumping!' Then his grin faded. 'Huh! They've gone again! Something

27

has definitely frightened them away. If anything's chasing them, I'd better go and help,' thought Bronty. He followed the tracks to where a spring of cool water bubbled from beneath a heap of rocks. His three friends were beside the spring, trying to remove the mud, leaves and thick dust from Bronty's gullumping. 'Right!' he smiled. 'It's time to gallump again! It will scare away whatever is chasing them.'

But as Bronty ran, the heap of rocks

over the spring shook, then collapsed as a powerful jet of water burst forth. Trisha, Steggy and Tyro danced as the spray blasted off the mud and leaves. 'Hurrah for Bronty! His gallumping came in handy after all!' they laughed. 'What about me?' wailed Bronty, from the top of the new fountain. 'Don't worry!' shouted the others. 'We'll rescue you as soon as we're clean again!'